All Night Arcade

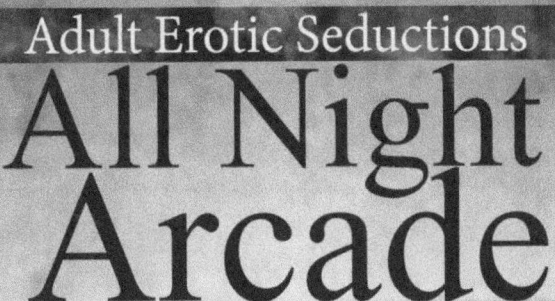

I0683470

Jack Ryder

WARNING

* * * * * * * * * * * * * * * * * *

WANT FREE COPIES OF MY BOOKS?
Just visit my blog and download free copies of my books:
jack-ryder.awesomeauthors.org/jack-ryder

About the Publisher

4Fun Publishing, a member of **BLVNP Incorporated**, 340 S. Lemon #6200, Walnut CA 91789, info@blvnp.com / legal@blvnp.com
NOTE: Due to the highly emotional reaction of some people to works of erotic fiction, any email sent to the above address that contains foul language or religious references is automatically deleted by our anti-spam software and will not be seen. All other communications are welcome.

DISCLAIMER

Please don't be stupid and kill yourself. This book is a work of FICTION. Do not try any new sexual practice that you find in this book. It is fiction and not to be confused with reality. Neither the author nor the publisher or its associates assume any responsibility for any loss, injury, death or legal consequences resulting from acting on the contents in this book. Every character in this book is over 18 years of age. The author's opinions are not to be construed as the opinions of the publisher. The material in this book is for entertainment purposes ONLY. Enjoy.

All Night Arcade
Adult Erotic Seductions

By: Jack Ryder

© Jack Ryder 2015
ISBN: 978-1-68030-482-4

Chapter 1

I have always enjoyed working at the arcade. Sort of a playground for adults so to speak. My wife Dana has never been real thrilled with my choice of employment. Especially since I work the night shift and don't get home till well after sunrise most mornings. Sometimes, not till after the lunch time hour.

I chose the night shift because you get much more "action" after dark! Usually a good mixed crowd of curious experimenters thrown together with a group of "here to play all night" folks. I usually do my best to see to it that the curiosity seekers have a good experience so they will want to return again...and again.

Sunday is the only day I have off. I would work that too if I were single, but the wife would cut my nuts off if I did not at least stay home ONE night each week. I have always found that each night has its own type of crowd. Monday is the lonely wife crowd. Tuesday and Thursday are the nights that are the slowest. But I fill that idle time by allowing the street girls to hang out and do what they do.

Friday and Saturday are the busiest nights and they keep me entertained best of all. Although the street girls do have a way of keeping me occupied on Tuesdays and Thursdays. But Wednesday night is what I have always called the mystery night. I am always busy but I just never know what is going to happen next or what kind of group will show up. It is sort of a "pot luck" crowd. And THAT can be very interesting!

Tonight was a typical Tuesday evening. I got most of my evening duties completed between 7 and 9pm as I normally do. During this time frame there is usually a slow shuffle of men that go back to the private booths to suck some cock through the glory holes. These are the wanna-be sort of men that are thrilled with the anonymity of having sex with other men without risking being seen by anyone else. Or having to admit to themselves that this thrills them so much.

It was just after nine when I saw her come into the front foyer leading into the main room. There are three separate areas in the arcade. The main room is the center part. It is where my customer counter is located. It is where the rows and rows of DVD racks are, the rows and rows of sexy apparel and the glass display counters with all the adult sex toys. There are four hidden cameras that cover the main area. The video screen is behind the counter where I can keep an eye on everything. I was watching her from all four angles as she slowly made her way towards me at the counter. She was gorgeous!

"My name's Dixie, Hun!" She was bent over the counter before I could stick out a hand to greet her properly. Her fluffy collared jacket fell open enough to expose her bare breasts to me. My eyes were riveted to her tits as she continued to look down into the glass like she was looking at the dildos in the case. "I'm new here and the other girls said you are nice to us working gals." Her eyes moved upward to catch me staring at her lovely 36CC globes.

Dixie placed her elbows on the glass but did not adjust her jacket or try to stand up. Her tits were nearly right in my face. "You gunna be nice to me, darlin?" She had a gleam in her eye as she said it and a subtle little grin. "I could be...so nice to you!" She reached over and laid her hand on my arm. "Do you get a break around this joint?" she whispered as she stood up but leather coat wide open. "Somewhere private...where we could...enjoy ourselves?"

Dixie pulled her jacket closed as we heard the doorbell dingle to announce the arrival of two younger men. They took a quick look at her but then hurried to the booths on the eastside of the building. Dixie was smiling sweetly as I dialed my cell phone. "George...can you...cover for me about an hour!" She was now petting my arm softly as I glanced down at her gorgeous shapely legs. The indecently short mini skirt barely covered her honey pot and her thighs looked yummy.

I sat down on the couch across from my desk as she opened her jacket and let it fall to the floor. "So, Dixie...what did you have in mind?" I teased her as I kicked off my shoes.

"I intend to rock your world!" she said it softly as she unzipped her skirt and let it fall to her ankles. Dixie was now standing in front of me in only her garter belt, black sheer stockings and stiletto heels. "That way you will always be willing to have me back!" She stepped right in front of me and I was looking straight up into her dripping wet gash.

"Oh, Dixie, look at that!" I whispered as I reached up to run a finger up her slit.

I quickly unfastened my jeans as Dixie bent down yanking them off when I raised my ass off the sofa. "And look at THAT!" She giggled cheerily as she saw my throbbing 8-inch prick. "I think I have just the right size slot to fit that peg!" She bent forward to suck my dick into her mouth as she shifted down onto her knees.

"Oooh, Dixie...Yessssss," I gasped my approval.

It was tremendously arousing to watch her gorgeous breasts swinging back and forth as her head bounced up and down. She looked so fucking sexy on her knees between my legs that it thrilled me to just sit back and watch her blowing me. Once she had me so excited that my legs were trembling, she scooted up and placed a condom on my prick with her mouth. "Oh God, that's sexy!" I moaned.

Dixie stood up and winked at me. "I bet you'll like this even more!" she said. After straddling my lap, she very slowly squatted down till my prick was buried inside of her. Then she very slowly stood back up and repeated it over and over. Squatting and lifting over and over very slowly. It was fantastically arousing as I could watch my dick slowly disappear and then come back out of her hole. I could see her pussy lips pull out as she lifted and then pressed in when she squatted. "Myyyyy God, that's sexy!" I groaned.

Smack, smack, smack, smack...when she increased the speed and force of her thrusts, her ass slapped down against my thighs and echoed off the walls of my office. "Oooh Yesss...Fuck Me, Baby, Fuck Me!" I moaned. Dixie had the most wonderful smile on her face as I bent forward to greedily suck on her gorgeous tits while she bounced up and down. "Yes, baby, take what you want," she whispered. That was all the invitation I needed!

I lifted Dixie up off my lap and placed her on her back. I pushed her feet all the way up by her head and then plowed back into her pussy till I was buried to the root. "Oooh Yes...Yes!" Dixie gasped as my cock invaded her much deeper than before. I could feel her quivering as I pounded into her very savagely. I reached down and twisted on one of her nipples as I felt the load building up in my balls. "Give it to me...Give it to me...Give it to me," she grunted. I shoved as far in as I could go and my legs trembled uncontrollably as my dick filled up the condom inside her hot sex.

"You can visit any time you like, Hunny!" I informed her as I pulled my jeans back on.

Dixie gave me a sweet little kiss before she left. "That was fun, Darlin'!" she whispered in my ear. "I am definitely going to want to do that again!" she added. I reached back and patted her delicious ass.

"I am definitely going to want some more of this too, baby!" I squeezed her left ass cheek gently. I showed her a pouty lip as she zipped up her jacket. "And lots more of those!"

I chuckled.

"Hey, Jake, your wife called!"

I grimaced as George yelled it across the room. Even though I'm sure that Dixie wouldn't give a shit if I'm married or not, I still dislike advertising my personal information inside the arcade. You never know what some of these men might be capable of. "I told her you were doing lunch," he taunted.

I heard Dixie chuckle at that as she was just going out the door. "Let's DO lunch on Thursday, Hun!" She called back before the door swung closed.

I called Dana just as soon as George returned to his work post. "I just wanted to know if you will be home in the morning or not," Dana informed me. I reached down to turn on the video feed of the hidden cameras that I have placed throughout our house. When the multi split screen came up, I could see that she was on our bed. She was naked and Bob, the 19-year-old boy from next door, was between her legs eating her pussy.

"I'll be late tomorrow, about noon," I told her. This would allow him to spend the night. THAT was the real reason for her call!

"You know how much I hate you working nights!" It came out almost as a moan. I could see that Bob was shoving his fingers up into her gash.

"Yes, dear. And I truly appreciate how well you deal with it." I was smiling to myself as I said it. I could very clearly see the lust on her face. "I better let you go now," I added as I saw him crawling forward to mount her. "Yes...I better...GO oooooh."

I hung up just as Bob shoved his dick into her cunt.

I have known for months that Dana is fucking other men sometimes. Bob, the kid from next door is just her latest boy toy diversion. I don't begrudge her these evening frolics. I get more pussy than I can shake a stick at. Though she has never come out and asked me about it, I am sure that she knows I have a hard time turning down pussy. Young or old. I just can't say no!

"Fiona...so happy you dropped by!" My voice sweet as candy. I knew for a fact that she would.

She always comes by to see me at midnight on Tuesday. She is always looking for a place to rest and a bed mate for when she goes home just before sunrise. "You can snooze in the office till I get off!" I suggested softly. "Then I am all yours till late afternoon...if you like."

Fiona came to the counter and kissed my cheek gently. "Gunna have some left for me?" she whispered as she flashed her tits at me. "I always have some left for you, Hunny."

I laughed.

I managed to get all my business responsibilities completed by 7am. Fiona was holding my hand as we left from the door in the back. Fiona was sucking on my dick as I pulled my car out of the alleyway and turned on the expressway that would lead to her trailer park. "You going to let me eat your pussy this morning?" I asked while she bounced up and down on my rigidness.

"No baby. I'm going to fuck you till we're so exhausted that we will both pass out after you cum."

Fiona lives in a very nice two bedroom trailer that is in a fairly upscale gated trailer park. She told me on my first visit here that her deceased husband left it to her in his will. It had been his secret love nest for many years. But now it is hers. She has also confided that he left her plenty of money to survive on.

At 38 years old, Fiona is a little older than most of the other working girls that hang out around the arcade. But she is still an absolute bombshell and there are lots of men who enjoy sex with an older woman. Fiona has confided that she really doesn't need the money. She jokes that it is the only way she can see me three nights each week. But it is obvious that the main reason she hangs out on the street is that she loves the sex. I have seen her fuck plenty of guys for free in the arcade booths in the back.

As always, Fiona cooked us breakfast and then we took a quick shower together. I love feeling my hands all over her slippery voluptuous body as we lather one another. She is a very healthy 38-26-36 and she keeps herself very firm and flexible with weekly yoga classes. She really is a sexy woman!

"You enjoyed watching me suck George off, huh?" she taunted as I crawled up onto the bed between her legs.

"Yes, I did," I mumbled it as I pressed my face between her thighs and began to slurp on her dripping gash.

"Ooooh, Jake, Ooooh Yes, Baby!" Her hands found my head and pushed my face deeper into her sex. "Oooooh, Jaaaaaaake!" It was a deep throaty moan.

I took my sweet ass time eating her. I love eating pussy and I especially like to tease and drag it out till she gets so desperately hungry that it feels exquisite when I finally scoot up and shove my dick inside. "Oooooh Jake, Pleeeeeze...pleeeeeze...fuck me...fuck me." Her head was thrashing back and forth as she groaned it. Her whole body was quivering as I slid up on top.

"Ooooooooh, Jaaaaake," she moaned loudly as my cock invaded her saucy hole. "Jaaaake!"

Smack, smack, smack, smack...my belly slammed down on top of hers as I drilled into her sex hard and fast. The look on her face was pure bliss and I loved how she stared into my eyes the entire time I was fucking her.

I pounded into Fiona like this for nearly ten minutes. Her pussy was contracting into climax so continuously that her fluid was squirting out all over our thighs and her body was jerking and writhing uncontrollably. I shoved all the way into her one last time and blew my load deep into her womb. "Oh Yes...Oh Yes...Oh Yes!" I bellowed with each spasm of my prick. We were both so exhausted that we drifted off to sleep within moments after I rolled off her and kissed her gently on the cheek.

Chapter 2

"Ooooh, Bobbie...Take Me...Take Me." Dana was thrilled with the fat hard dick that was invading the innermost reaches of her sex. The sounds of his soft grunted moans of pleasure were very satisfying for her.

Her legs were spread wide open for him. Inviting him to press further and further into her dripping wet hole. But there was an ache in her heart. She could remember when it was Jake that was this hungry for her. She could remember when it was his slippery sweaty body that was writhing on top of her. It was his voice that moaned her name. It was his hot sticky seed that sprayed into her pussy.

"Oh Dana...Dana...Ooooh Dana!" His dick began to spasm and Dana could feel the heat of his load filling her vagina.

"Yes, Baby...give it to me, baby...give it to me." She ran her fingers through his hair as he emptied his semen into her.

Dana enjoys the fact that she is the only woman that Bobbie has ever been with. She had seduced him one evening several months ago after asking him over to fix the faucet in the bath room for the master bedroom. He had been so thrilled to give up his virginity. It had been so endearing that she has allowed him to come over and fuck her twice a week ever since.

Bobbie rolled off and scooted up to spoon with her from behind. Deep in her heart, Dana wished that it was Jake's hands that were now fondling her breasts. She wished that it was his seed that was slowly oozing out of her pussy.

"Maybe you should go home now...before your mother misses you," she whispered it softly. She said it partly just to get him out of the house. But it was also a reminder to herself that he is way too young to get too involved with.

Dana slept late that Wednesday morning. By the time she ate breakfast and took her shower, it was nearing noon and Jake was still not home yet. As she was getting dressed to go to her pilates class, she noticed that her black negligee was still lying on the floor next to the bed. At first, she thought about picking it up and putting it in the laundry. Especially since there was the strong musky odor of sex on it and cum stains from where Bobbie's cum had oozed out. Then, she decided to leave it there for Jake to see.

"Maybe it will shake him up and get his attention!" She decided in her mind. She reached down and lifted the nightie up onto the bed where he would be sure to notice it.

***

Dana was not around when I got home at half past two on Wednesday afternoon. There was a note that said she would be gone till dinner time. Since I had only gotten about four hours of sleep after banging Fiona, I decided to take a nap till dinner time. I saw the black nightie lying across the bed. I saw the cum stains all over it.

I smiled as I picked it up and took it to the laundry basket. I couldn't help but wonder if she had left it there to taunt me or if she had simply forgotten it was there. I have noticed over the last several months that she has gotten more careless about her "secret" nighttime affairs. I have sometimes found cigarette butts in the ashtray that don't belong to me. I have found used condoms on the floor next to the bed. I have found huge wet spots on the bed sheets.

"Anything interesting happen today?" Dana smiled coyly as she asked it. I nearly dropped my fork as I tried to act like nothing was out of the ordinary. I have noticed that she also likes to try to get a rise out of me. Usually at dinner or just before I am ready to go to work. I told her it had just been another normal Wednesday. She seemed unhappy that I did not mention the nightie.

Wednesday night seemed to drag on as most do. The crowd that night was mostly men who were there to play with each other back in the theater section. Occasionally, a couple of younger and more inhibited men would make eyes at each other as they browsed through the gay porn section and then disappear back into the private booth area where they could suck each other off through the privacy of the glory holes.

I had monitored the secret cameras at home throughout the evening. I was surprised that Dana had left the house about 8pm and still had not returned now that it was closing in on midnight. I was beginning to worry about her. Although she has been having sex with other men at home, she is not the sort of woman that is used to going out and dealing with the creeps in the world. Until now, all the men she has had sex with were from around the neighborhood or fellas that she met at the grocery store.

It was about ten past midnight when I saw the lights come on in the living room at home. At the time, there were just a couple of men back in the theater playing with each other and George had just left for his lunch break.

I could tell by the way that Dana was moving that she was probably a bit drunk. I could also tell that she was quite horny by the way she was rubbing herself all over the two men that she had brought home with her.

The men were just beginning to strip Dana in the middle of my living room when Dixie sauntered in. "Would you care for some company, Hunny?" The short red mini skirt that she had on barely covered the garter snaps holding up her black fishnet stockings. Her sexy legs looked fabulous as she stepped towards me. As she removed the matching red vest jacket, I could see her gorgeous breasts through the white chiffon blouse.

One of the men was now sucking on Dana's tits while the other man was on the floor with his face buried in the crack of her ass lapping away at her pussy. "Come here, baby. Take a look at this," I invited her with a chuckle.

"Someone you know, Jake?" Dixie asked when she glanced down at the screen. I already had her tits cupped in my hands as she bent over to see the screen.

"That's my wife Dana." I chuckled as I rubbed her nipples through the soft fabric of her blouse. "As you can see...she keeps herself entertained while I'm hard at work." I pressed forward so Dixie could feel my rigid prick against the crack of her butt.

"Yes, you certainly are hard...at work," Dixie laughed her reply. I let go of her tits and lifted her skirt up to expose her bare ass. "Are you up for a little risk?" I pulled my sweat pants down and dragged my dick up and down her crack.

"Yes, Hunny...fuck me right here," she purred as I slipped my dick up into her gash. On the screen, Dana was bent over the arm of the couch. One man was behind her on his knees plowing away at her pussy. The other man was in front of her and she was sucking him off while he mashed her tits with both hands. "Yes...give it to me good," Dixie moaned as I placed both hands on her hips and began to ram into her from behind.

Smack, smack, smack, smack...my belly was slapping against her ass when we heard the ding of the doorbell. Two fellas walked in and glanced over at us. I never stopped drilling into Dixie as they smiled and then made their way back to the private booths. "I like this risk thing," she giggled as I reached forward to mash on her tits some more.

"Me too, Bab. Me too!" I panted.

"Fuck me...Fuck me...Fuck me." Her moans came out as grunts as I pounded into her over and over. On the screen, the man in front had just yanked his dick out of Dana's mouth and was spraying his cum all over her face and tits. "Oh, she's a nasty girl," Dixie murmured as she saw Dana smearing the cum all over her face with the man's cock.

The doorbell jingled again as I continued to slam my cock into Dixie's gushing wet hole. Two men and one of the working girls from down the street entered. "Theater is on the house," I gasped loud enough for them to hear. That would allow her to service both men with a small group of onlookers. I never missed a stroke as they slowly walked past us towards the theater entrance.

My cock felt like it swelled even harder as they watched me fucking Dixie while they strolled past. I'm certain that it aroused Dixie as well. I felt a large gush of fluid as she saw all of them gawking at us.

Squish, squish, squish, squish. I was ramming into Dixie harder and faster as we watched the guy fucking Dana pull his dick out and spray his load all over her ass and lower back. "Oh God, Yes...Oh Yes...Oh yes." Dixie was climaxing so forcefully that her pussy muscles felt like a vibrator milking my prick. I shoved myself in one last time and my legs were quivering as I shot my cum deep into Dixie's gripping hole.

"Oh fuck yes," I groaned as I gazed at my wife on the screen with cum all over her.

"That was really hot!" Dixie panted as I pulled my dick out of her and she stood back up.

As soon as Dixie left, I turned my full attention on Dana. She was again masturbating to get herself off after her little romp with the men. I was fascinated that she had to manually get herself off after having fucked those two men. I sort of felt bad for her in a way. She seems to be trying so hard to achieve something. And yet, it seems just out of reach somehow.

Chapter 3

I was really busy on Thursday night. From the time I started at 7pm my attention was kept busy watching the working girls that brought a steady stream of Johns in to bang back in the private booths. I had been so busy watching the corridor to ensure the girls safety that I had not taken the time to check on the cameras from home. I noticed that the light was on in the living room but she was not at home.

About a quarter after 9pm, I heard the front door bell ring. When I looked up, I saw a very gorgeous young woman stroll in. She appeared to smile a little as she slowly made her way over to the aisle between the porn magazines and videos. She was stunning. With the four inch heels that she was wearing, she looked like she'd be about 5 foot 10. Her long shapely legs were encased by sheer black nylons and with the shortness of her mini skirt, those legs seemed to go on forever.

Her very long silky black hair was obviously a wig. But it was one of those very expensive ones that reached all the way down to her waist and the bangs were cut straight across her forehead. I could not see her eyes because she was wearing very large round sun glasses that were just dark enough to conceal her eyes. Her transparent black chiffon blouse allowed a very clear view of her milky white tits through the fabric. I kept her in view long enough to get a good gawk at her. I felt a bit of a wiggle as I wondered how it would be to suck on those luscious white tits.

It was only a few moments before a man on the other side of the room slowly made his way over to her side. At that moment, she was paging through a skin magazine and I watched as he fondled her ass while he glanced over her shoulder to see what she was looking at. I noticed that her body shivered a bit as he rubbed her ass and whispered something in her ear. She placed the magazine back on the rack and slowly strolled back to the private room area.

She slipped into the very first booth and left the door open. The man followed her back moments later and entered the same booth. He closed the door behind him. Within a few minutes, I could hear the slapping noises of skin smacking against skin and a low lustful moaning coming from the booth. That was followed a couple of minutes later by a very loud groan. Then it was silent.

When the man came out of the booth, he stopped at the magazine rack to whisper something to the man that was standing there paging through a skin magazine. As the first man left, the other man quickly shoved the magazine back onto the rack and practically ran back to booth number one. Again there was slapping noises and moaning. While he was in the booth fucking the tall gorgeous woman, another six young men piled in the front door and made a beeline for the private area. They all quickly found a booth and I saw the lights come on when they pumped some money into slots for the video porn screens.

Over the next hour or so I watched one man after the other disappear into her booth as soon as one left. It was half past 11pm when Fiona walked in and sauntered up to the counter. "Anything new, Darling?" she whispered as she leaned over the counter to kiss my cheek. "Just the woman in back that has banged about eight or nine men," I chuckled. "Other than that, it's dead in here," I teased.

It was several minutes after the last man left before the woman in back finally came back out to the front. It seemed like she was gawking at Fiona as she very slowly made her way to the front door. I could very clearly see cum stains on the front of her dress and there was a river of jism running down both her legs as she opened the door. Just before she stepped outside, she turned and blew me a kiss. Then she was gone.

"What the hell was that?" Fiona laughed.

"I think she was sweet on you, baby." I chuckled my reply. "Didn't you see how she was checking you out as she walked through?" I squeezed Fiona's rump as I teased her. "I bet she knew you could satisfy her better than any of those men did," I taunted.

"Shut up and call George...I want to fuck you right now!" Fiona squeezed my butt as I made the call to the back. When George came up front, he told me to take my time because there was no one back in the theater and no one in the private area. I turned off the video feed from my house and just put it on record. I did not have the time to go back and review the footage from this evening. I would have to wait till I was through with Fiona.

After watching the mystery woman over the last couple of hours, I was hard as a brick as I opened the office couch into its sleeper bed. "Oh God, you are delicious," I groaned at Fiona as I watched her remove her mini skirt and chiffon blouse. "Bring those big beautiful tits here," I commanded her as I removed my jeans. Fiona came over and pressed me down onto my back and bent forward so her tits were in my face as she straddled me. "Yesss, Yesss," she purred softly as I greedily sucked back and forth on each of her breasts.

It felt wonderful that her pussy was dripping her arousal down onto my thighs while I sucked and mauled on her tits. "I want your dick in me," Fiona whispered it as she reached down to guide my prick into her juicy gash. "Yesss, Oh God, Yesss," she moaned. Squeak, squeak, squeak, squeak... the bed springs screamed in protest as Fiona pounded herself down onto my throbbing prick. I continued to pinch and pull on her nipples while she humped up and down.

"You wanted to fuck that nasty little whore, didn't you?" Her voice was a delightful taunt as she rode my cock.

"Yes...Yes I did," I panted. "I wanted to shove my cock up that juicy little cunt," I growled. I could feel more fluid oozing from Fiona's slit. "You'd like that, Hun." I squeezed even harder on her tits. "You'd love to see my dick impaling that nasty little whore...wouldn't you?"

Fiona's body began to jerk as her climax exploded inside of her. "YES...Oh God Yes...God Yes," she screamed. I twisted cruelly on her nipples as my dick emptied itself deep into her gushing snatch. Her whole body was twitching as my cock shot off four wads of semen into her.

"There you go, baby...that's what you really wanted," I teased her. Fiona fell forward and kissed me hungrily.

"God, I love fucking you, Jake," she gasped.

I left Fiona to sleep in the office while I completed my shift. When George came back from lunch, I was busy cleaning cum puddles off the private area floor in booth number one where my mystery woman had taken on nine different men. I did not hear George come back in. When I came back to the counter, I heard squeaking in the back. I decided to peek through the curtains to see what was up.

Fiona was on her stomach and George was on top of her driving himself into her even though she wasn't fully awake. "Get it over with, George." Her voice sounded annoyed. Smack, smack, smack, smack...he just continued to pound away at her even though she was clearly unhappy with him.

"Oh Yes...Oh Yes...Ooooh Yes!" George bellowed as he spewed his cum into her pussy.

"Next time, wait till I'm awake, asshole!" Fiona was very pissed as she shoved George off of her. I glared at him as he made his way past me.

"Not cool, shithead!" I growled at him.

It was nearly 2am when the phone rang. "You coming home in the morning?" It was Dana. I had been so busy playing with Fiona that I had forgotten to call her before I went to clean up the puddle in room number one.

"Depends, baby...do you want me to come home?" I teased her.

Usually, when she calls me like this, it's because she has something in mind.

There was a short pause before she answered me. "I was a bad girl this evening...a very dirty, nasty girl." She hesitated a moment for that to sink in. "I need you to punish me for my sleazy ways." It almost sounded like a giggle. I knew it would disappoint Fiona if I did not come home with her, but my dick was wiggling and it has been quite a while since Dana has requested my sexual attention.

"I'll be home as soon as my shift is over," I replied.

"Good, I'll be waiting for you," she whispered. "I need a good fucking!" she added.

After we finished our conversation, I went back and reviewed the video feed from my secret cameras at home. I was stunned by what I saw. She did not have anyone come over to fuck her this evening. She had no company at all. I watched as she took a shower, applied makeup to her face and painted her fingernails bright red. I watched her slowly put on a pair of sheer black nylons that she attached to a black garter belt. She did not bother to put on panties.

My eyes were beginning to bug out as I watched her put on a very short black mini skirt and then a transparent black chiffon blouse. My legs buckled and I had to sit down on the stool behind me as I watched her put on a very expensive long hair black wig. She gazed at herself in the mirror and smiled broadly as she then put on a pair of very large, round sunglasses. Dana had been the mystery woman who had fucked nine men in booth number one this evening. She was the nasty whore I fantasized about when I was fucking Fiona earlier. My entire body ached to go home and fuck her senseless.

I awoke Fiona at 6am. She was disappointed when I told her that my plans have changed for this morning's activities. But she was soon very pleased when I told her what I had in mind. She quickly went home to shower, spruce herself up and get changed. She would be waiting for me as soon as I got off work. She kissed me very passionately before she left.

"This is going to be so incredible!" she whispered.

Chapter 4

Fiona was waiting for me in the parking garage when I got off work. As I approached, she held open her knee length mink coat to show me she was completely nude underneath. "See something you like?" she giggled as I gawked at her gorgeous naked body.

"Every inch, baby... I love every inch," I answered. I got a terrific view of her smooth shaved pussy as she swung her legs into the passenger side of my car. "You look good enough to eat," I whispered it as I leaned in to kiss her cheek.

"You better!" she shot back with a chuckle.

There was a note on the kitchen table when we got to the house. *"In the bedroom...in the bed, in my nightie...hurry up!"* Fiona let out a cute belly laugh when I passed the note for her to read. "I love a girl who knows what she wants," Fiona whispered as I led her up the hall to my bedroom.

I paused for a moment to give her a quick kiss before we got to the doorway.

"Let's rock her world, baby," I whispered.

I was delighted when I saw Dana on the bed. She was wearing a black transparent baby doll nightie. She was also wearing that same expensive long hair black wig. She looked so fucking sexy. It was like having an entirely new wife in my bed. "I brought you a surprise, Hunny," I announced as I led Fiona to the bed. "But first, you must be punished...for that brazen display at the arcade tonight." I saw a hint of a smile curl onto her lips as I said it.

"This is Fiona, Luv." I unzipped my pants and let them fall to the floor. "You are going to watch her suck me off." This time it was me that smiled as Fiona let her mink coat fall to the floor and then bent down to take my dick in her mouth. "If you are a good girl, maybe I'll let you play with her when she's done."

I could see that Dana was trembling from her arousal as she watched Fiona slurping on my prick. I reached down and ran my fingers through her lovely blonde hair as I watched Dana begin to masturbate while her eyes were glued to Fiona's lips engulfing my cock over and over.

"That's it, baby. Get that cunt nice and juicy wet for me," I growled at her. It thrilled me as she glanced up and our eyes met. "If you're really good...maybe I'll fuck you when Fiona is done with you," I told her softly.

I saw Dana shudder as a wave of climax coursed through her. I reached down to hold Fiona's head and began to hump my cock into her mouth. Gluck, Gluck, Gluck, Gluck. Fiona made gagging noises as I rammed my dick further and further into her throat. Huge strands of precum and saliva oozed out onto Fiona's tits each time she lifted her head. I could see the deep lust in Dana's face while she watched Fiona sucking and jerking my dick.

As I was getting close to climax, I reached over and slipped three fingers up into Dana's sloppy wet gash. "Oooh God, yesssss," Dana gasped. I could feel the load racing to the tip of my dick as I drilled my fingers in and out her.

"Now, baby...Now!" I screamed. Fiona pulled my dick out of her mouth and jerked me off till I spewed my cum all over her tits.

"Oooh Yes...Oooh yes." Dana moaned as she climaxed too. I felt a gush of fluid as her pussy clenched at my intruding fingers. "Oooh Jake, Oooh Jaaaaake." It was a deep husky moan.

Dana was still jerking and shuddering as Fiona climbed onto the bed and crawled up so her tits were in Dana's face. "If you clean all this mess off my tits, maybe I'll eat your nasty little cunt for you."

Without hesitation, Dana lifted her head and started licking and sucking all the cum off Fiona's breasts. "Yesss...that's it...that's it, Hun." Fiona gently held Dana's face as she fed her cum drenched tits to her.

I walked around and sat on the other side of the bed next to them and watched as Fiona scooted up and locked into a deep passionate kiss with Dana. It thrilled me to see my wife's hands roaming all over Fiona's gorgeous voluptuous body. To watch her hungrily kissing another woman. Fondling her, petting her. My dick began to wiggle back to life as I saw Dana slip her fingers up into Fiona's wet slit. "Yes, baby...Yesssss," Fiona whispered.

Fiona pulled Dana to the middle of the bed and squatted over her face. "I'll eat your pussy if you'll eat mine," she taunted her as she lowered her gash onto Dana's mouth. I saw Dana's hands come up to Fiona's ass as she began to greedily lap at Fiona's drenched pussy. My dick was throbbing between my legs as Fiona lowered her head to chew on my wife's drenched muff.

"Oh my God," I groaned softly as I began to stroke my cock.

It was deliciously erotic and arousing to listen to the hungry slurping sounds they made as they ate each other out. It was thrilling to hear their deep guttural moans of pleasure, the deep breathy gasps of lust. I rolled off the bed and scooted up behind Fiona. It was electrifying to glance down and see my wife eating my mistress's cunt so ravenously.

***

Dana was amazed by how ecstatic she felt as she watched Jake's cock burrow into another woman's cunt. *"This is the Jake I have been waiting for,"* she thought to herself as she felt his balls gently graze her nose. Dana had found the "secret" cameras several months ago and has been systematically fucking every guy in the neighborhood. She has been desperately trying to get his attention.

Dana had been confounded by the fact that Jake has never said a word about her fucking these other men. Tonight had been a last ditch attempt to get his attention once and for all. "Yes, fuck me, Jake...Fuck me." Dana felt her pussy gush as Fiona moaned Jake's name. Dana had seen the tall gorgeous blonde all over Jake at the arcade last night. She had secretly hoped that Jake would bring her home someday. She never expected that she would lying here eating her cock filled snatch this morning.

"You were a very bad girl tonight," Jake grunted as he humped his dick all the way into Fiona's sloppy wet gash. "This is just the beginning, you little wench." He reached down to place his dick into Dana's mouth for a couple of thrusts before shoving back into Fiona. Squish, squish, squish, squish....as Jake pounded into Fiona, the juices squirted out all over Dana's face. "Yes, baby...I want to be your slut," Dana moaned as Fiona fingered her to climax. "Oh Yessss...God Yes," she moaned loudly.

***

When I heard Dana climaxing, I had Fiona roll onto her back and told Dana to get on her knees so she could finish Fiona off with her fingers and tongue. "Better make her happy." I laughed wickedly as I rammed my dick into Dana's quivering snatch. "She will be spending a lot of time in our bed from now on." I felt Dana vibrate as I savagely slapped her ass cheeks.

"Oooh, Jake...this bitch is good," Fiona groaned throatily. I felt the gush of fluid from Dana's pussy as she heard Fiona's praise. It electrified me to watch Dana greedily eating Fiona's pussy. My legs were vibrating as I slammed into Dana over and over. "Oooooh God, Yesssss...Yesss," Fiona screamed as her body jerked into orgasm.

"Fuck Yes...Fuck Yes...Fuck Yes," I bellowed my reply. I could feel Dana writhing into another climax as I filled her pussy with my hot thick jism.

It felt fabulous to fall asleep sandwiched between my wife and my mistress. Not only had Dana accepted Fiona into our bed, she had welcomed it and participated greedily. I drifted off to sleep with a huge grin on my face. Dana was spooned up against my belly and Fiona was behind me with her tits pressed against my back. I slept very soundly.

It was just past 3pm when I awoke to the glorious sensation of a hot, wet mouth sucking my dick. "There you are, baby," Fiona lifted her head to smile at me. "You wanna cum in my mouth? Or should I climb on this big beautiful cock?" she giggled.

"Fuck me...Oh pleeeeeze...Fuck me," I moaned my reply.

Dana was no longer in the bed with us. By the wonderful smells coming from the kitchen, I could tell that she was out there cooking us lasagna for dinner. "Dana said I could fuck you any time I want," Fiona informed me as she scooted up to mount my throbbing prick.

"Oooh God, yes! That's good...that's good," I groaned my reply.

Squeak, squeak, squeak, squeak...The bed springs groaned beneath us as Fiona forcefully bounced up and down on my rigidness. Out of the corner of my eye, I noticed a movement over in the doorway. When I turned my head, I saw Dana standing there with her hand between her legs. She had her white satin robe pulled open and she was masturbating while she watched Fiona's pussy pounding up and down on my prick.

"Ooooh, Jaaaaaake, your cock feels so good!"

I saw Dana shudder into a small climax as she heard Fiona's husky moan.

"Yes, baby...Fuck Me...Fuck Me," I moaned. Dana shuddered again as she used her other hand to pull on her own nipples. I could feel the load swelling in my nuts as Dana continued to finger herself to a series of small orgasms. "Here it is, baby...here it is," I screamed it as my cock exploded deep into Fiona's sloppy gash. As my semen spewed into her, I felt Fiona begin to vibrate into a powerful orgasm too. Dana was pressed against the doorway as her body jerked and twitched.

"Dinner will...be ready....in twenty minutes," Dana panted.

At dinner, Dana made a quiet announcement. "I have invited Fiona to visit any time she likes." She had a coy smile on her face as she said it.

Fiona had an announcement too. "And I have told Dana that she can come hang out on the street with me...any time she likes."

I have to confess that the thought of my wife screwing other men for money was a little disturbing. But I also was getting painfully erect just thinking about it too. I had the sudden vision of her black dress covered in semen when she left the arcade last night.

"And where does that leave me?" I tried not to sound too anxious. "Does that mean I will be sleeping alone now?" I asked it softly. They both laughed loudly.

"Silly man! That means you will have your hands very full from now on!" Fiona was the one who answered.

"We plan to share you together...and separately," Dana added with a giggle. I was going to ask if banging other men would dull their appetite for me. But then I remembered how horny Fiona gets after she's had a good night. I decided to keep that to myself.

***

It was just past midnight on Friday when Dana and Fiona both came into the arcade together.

I was in the office fucking Dixie when they sauntered past George at the counter and just came straight back into my office. Dixie was bouncing up and down on my lap when I heard them giggling.

"Who's that, Hun?" Dixie gasped as she glanced over and saw them standing inside the room with us.

"My wife and my mistress," I growled. I did not stop sucking on her tits.

"Oooh, Jake...Where can I... sign up for that?" Dixie panted as she continued to thrust up and down on my prick.

I glanced over at them and they were both smiling. Fiona was behind Dana. She was kissing the back of Dana's neck and fondling her tits as she winked at me.

"You'll have to get their permission for that, Hun," I replied as I reached up to twist on one of Dixie's pebble hard nipples.

"Oooh yes...please...pleeeeeeeze," Dixie gasped in a deep throaty moan.

Dana and Fiona made their way over to us and each of them reached down to fondle one of Dixie's breasts as she continued to impale herself on my dick. "Can you keep him happy when we are busy?" Dana asked softly as she bent forward to kiss the side of Dixie's neck while she twisted on one of her nipples.

"Oh Yes...Oh Yes...Oh Yes," Dixie panted her reply, never even missing a stroke as she humped me savagely.

Fiona reached down and pulled Dixie's right hand up between her legs underneath her mini skirt. "Can you keep US happy when HE is busy?" Fiona murmured as she began to hump herself on Dixie's fingers.

"Oh yes...oh yes...I'm Cumming...I'm Cumming...Oh God Yes!" Dixie screamed her reply. As Dixie started to shudder and vibrate on my cock, I erupted deep into her and flooded her with three huge wads of semen. Dana and Fiona were both grinning as I softly moaned while my entire body jerked through my climax.

When I glanced down, I saw that Dixie had shoved her other hand up between Dana's legs and she was finger fucking them both now. It only took a few more moments before they both got off and shuddered as she brought them to orgasm. "Yes...you are welcome...to play with us," Dana panted softly as she held Dixie's hand motionless with her fingers still buried in her gash.

I left the three of them in the office when I went out to relieve George. "Think you can handle three horny women?" I chuckled as he peeked into the back. They were all on the pull out couch bed kissing and fondling each other...completely naked.

"Oh God, I'd love to try," he gasped his answer. Over the next hour I heard many husky moans and George squealing like a little girl as they teased and tortured him for a very long time before they let him climax. When he came back out, he looked like he had just run the Boston marathon.

Within a month, both Fiona and Dixie moved in with Dana and me. We worked it out so each of them slept alone with me twice each week. And on Sunday, the four of us all slept together and spent the entire day doing things all together. I gotta tell you that I am the luckiest guy on Earth to have three lovely working girls lavishing their love and attention on me 24/7!

--- End ---

Here is a sample from another story you may enjoy:

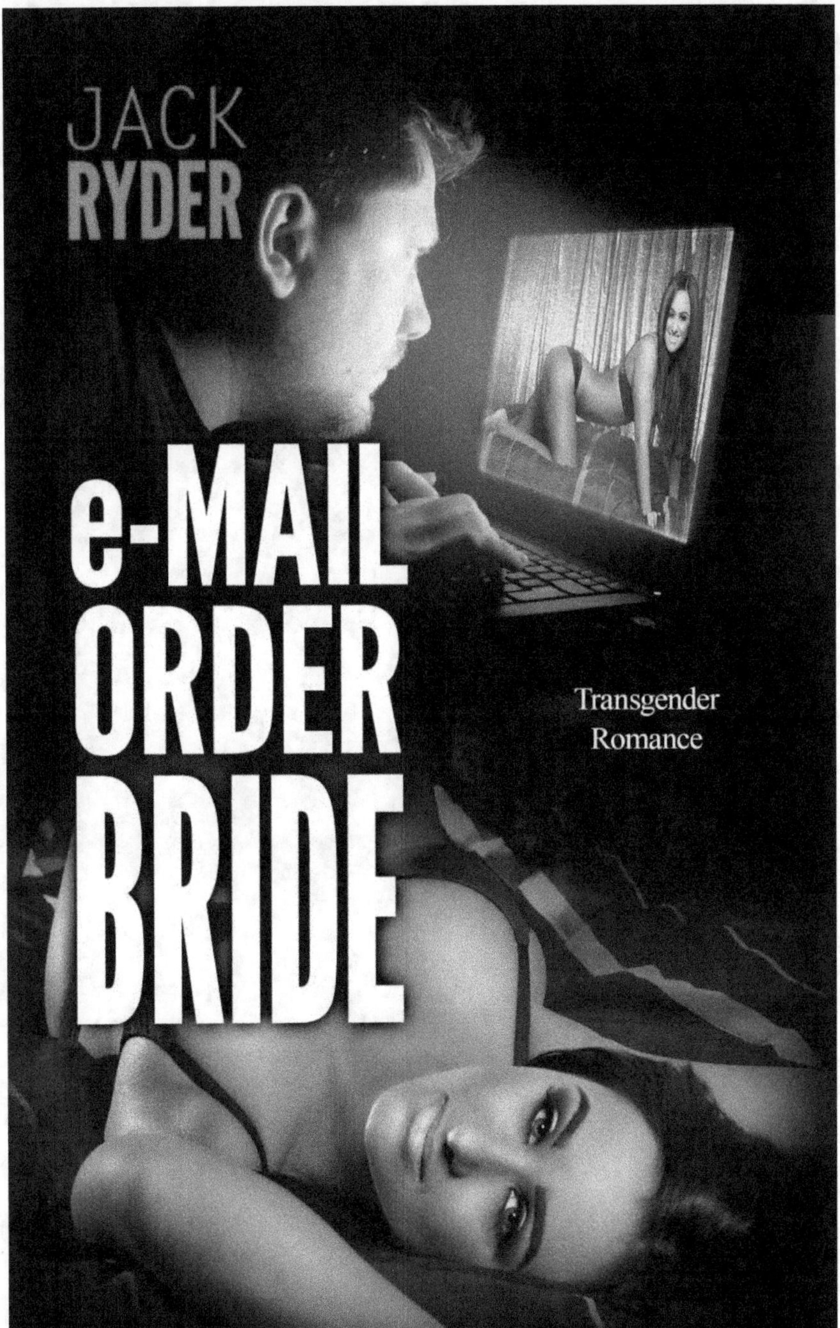
JACK
RYDER
e-MAIL
ORDER
BRIDE
Transgender
Romance

Seatac was a mad house at 9pm on a Friday night. I was glad that I had left early so I had plenty of time to deal with the sports traffic on I-5 due to the Mariners Game. Then I had to deal with the security checks to make my way to the proper air terminal gate for Sam's arrival. I made it to the gate with ten minutes to spare. I felt an overwhelming giddiness as I watched her airplane pull up to the loading dock.

"Ooooh, Fuck me," I gasped beneath my breath as I saw her coming down the ramp. She was wearing a white tube dress that fit her like a second skin. It was so short that I could see the bottom inch of her white panties as she walked towards me. She was wearing a big round black hat and her long black hair was in a tight braided ponytail. She had huge dark sunglasses on and was smiling broadly as she got closer and closer. Her long muscular legs looked fabulous.

"You are even more gorgeous in person," she told me in that wonderfully husky voice as she bent forward to kiss one cheek and then the other.

"Oh Sam...You look gorgeous," I groaned my reply. It thrilled me to see all the heads turning as we made our way to the baggage claim to get her luggage. And even more when she reached down to hold my hand as we waited at the turnstile.

"Ha-ha-ha-ha, I should have guessed that you would have a Hummer," Sam giggled when I pointed out my forest green Humvee.

"It was my divorce present to myself," I informed her as I opened the passenger door. "And my cabin in the hills was the other." My dick wiggled as she swung her legs into the vehicle. I got a quick glance of her white panties and a great look down the top of her dress at her tits. Her nipples were just as hard as last night.

"I have something to tell you before we get to the hotel." She said it very softly as we were pulling out of the parking garage. "I make porn movies, Bobby...I am a porn Queen in Russia."

I glanced over at her and she was gazing at me intently. "Wow, Sam...How did I ever get so lucky?" My voice sort of trembled a bit. "I'm even more amazed that you have an interest in me now."

I felt her hand rest gently on my thigh as I turned my attention back to driving the vehicle. "I think that I may be the lucky one," she whispered it softly. "I came here to see you because there is something I need to show you." She said it so softly that I could barely hear her. "I have a feeling about you...that it will be okay." Her hand gently brushed up and down my thigh. I could feel my dick throbbing in my jeans. "You have no idea how much I hope I am right," she added.

I couldn't keep my eyes off of Sam while she was checking in at the hotel. Neither could any of the other men in the front lobby area. By the time we made it to the elevator, several of the bell hops and a couple of the men from the lobby had asked Sam for her autograph. Except they knew her by the name Samantha Bone.

I could tell that Sam was a bit annoyed and upset as the elevator started to rise towards the penthouse suite. "It bothers me that all those men knew who I am and have seen me naked," she whispered it softly. "But you haven't yet." She sort of hung her head as she finished.

I reached over and held her hand gently. "I'm sure that whatever you are worrying about will be okay," I told her as I squeezed her hand. "I've been told that I am a fairly progressive sort of man." I chuckled.

Sam turned to face me and gave me a half smile. "I certainly hope you are, Hun," she answered me.

As soon as were in the penthouse suite, Sam kicked off her white heels and tossed her black hat onto the easy chair near the kitchen. She sat her sunglasses on the counter then reached up to grab a bottle of vodka from the top cabinet.

"Oh Geezus," I gasped as I gazed at her ass sticking out under her tight dress as it pulled up in back.

Sam poured the vodka into two 4 oz. tumblers then carried them and the bottle back into the living room. "Sit on the couch and be comfortable," she told me as she handed me one of the drinks. After she slammed down her entire drink, she pointed to mine. "Bottoms up...Hun," she giggled. As soon as I swallowed mine down, she refilled both tumblers and then stepped back about two feet from the couch.

"Moment of truth," she chuckled softly. Standing directly in front of me, she slowly pulled down the top of her tight dress until her tits were fully exposed to me. "Oooh Sam," I gasped. I could feel my pecker swelling in my jeans as I glanced at her gorgeous tits.

"The reason I didn't tell you about the porn movies is that I was afraid that you might ask me what sort of porn." She said it as she wiggled her dress down to her feet and kicked it off. I could now see that she wasn't wearing white panties, it was a white bikini bottom.

"You are so gorgeous, Sam," I moaned as I gawked at her beautiful body.

"Yes...but you haven't seen all of me yet," she whispered as she pulled the strings on her bikini and it fell off.

What she had on underneath the bikini I had never seen before. It was like a thong. But not quite a thong. It was a small fabric cup sort of thing with a thong strap in the center that went up the crack of her ass. There was a thick string that wrapped around her waist and tied to the center fabric in back. "This is what you haven't seen," she said it timidly as she reached behind to untie the string.

As the tiny cup fell to the floor, I was stunned and exhilarated at the same instant. My eyes were riveted between her legs at the perfect six inch flaccid cock. "Ooooh Sam," I whispered. "That is so...extraordinary." I could feel my dick throbbing.

"It's....okay?" Sam cooed as her eyes lifted up to peer into mine.

"Oh Sam, it's better than okay...it is...wonderful! I want to feel it get hard in my hand this first time," I whispered as I reached forward to gently fondle her perfect six inch dick...

If you enjoyed this sample then look for **E-Mail Order Bride**.

Also by this Author:

The Handyman Seduction

The Beer Bust Scandal

Scandalous Emotion

Intimate Relation

The Seduction of Kimi

Erotic Goes Hi-Tech

One at a Time

The Wizard Casey's Coven

The Inn Keeper's Wizard: When Love and Magic Collide

Trailer Trash Payback

Queer Intentions

Zoe's Fun House

Public Display

Test Drive

Breaking the Bonds

Trailer Trash Payback

The Hero's Welcome

The Twenty-Eight Day Cure

The Cougar Club

From the Author

WANT FREE COPIES OF MY BOOKS?
Just visit my blog and download free copies of my books:
jack-ryder.awesomeauthors.org/jack-ryder

If you have any comments, suggestions, or would just like to get a little personal, please feel free to email me at:
jack_ryder@awesomeauthors.org

If you enjoyed any of my books then please share the love and click like on my books in Amazon.

If you write me a review and send me an email I will send you a free book, or many.
(Just know that these emails are filtered by my publisher.)

Good news is always welcome.

One Last Thing, For Kindle Readers...

When you turn the page, Kindle will give you the opportunity to rate this book and share your thoughts on Facebook and Twitter. If you enjoyed my writings, would you please take a few seconds to let your friends know about it? Because... when they enjoy they will be grateful to you and so will I.

Thank You!

Jack Ryder
jack_ryder@awesomeauthors.org

About the Author

Jack Ryder LOVES everything there is about sex!

When he is not involved with his "swinger" friends, enjoying a steamy threesome, or being part of a raunchy "gang bang", you can find him on first class planes, trains, and cruise ships. Traveling seems to be the BEST way to finding new and interesting sexmates for him. Sexmates. Plural. He lives with the saying "The More, The Merrier!"

He owns a successful business in New York. He writes as a hobby and also as sort of documentation of his mind-blowing sexcapades over the years. He is presently roaming around the streets of Manhattan but can be anywhere in the world too, since he travels often. So, beware! You just might be his next mate.

"The most fun thing I enjoy when writing my stories is trying to figure out which is fantasy and which was memory. ENJOY! (Preferably with a friend. *wink*)" -Jack Ryder-

You may also like the books by these authors:

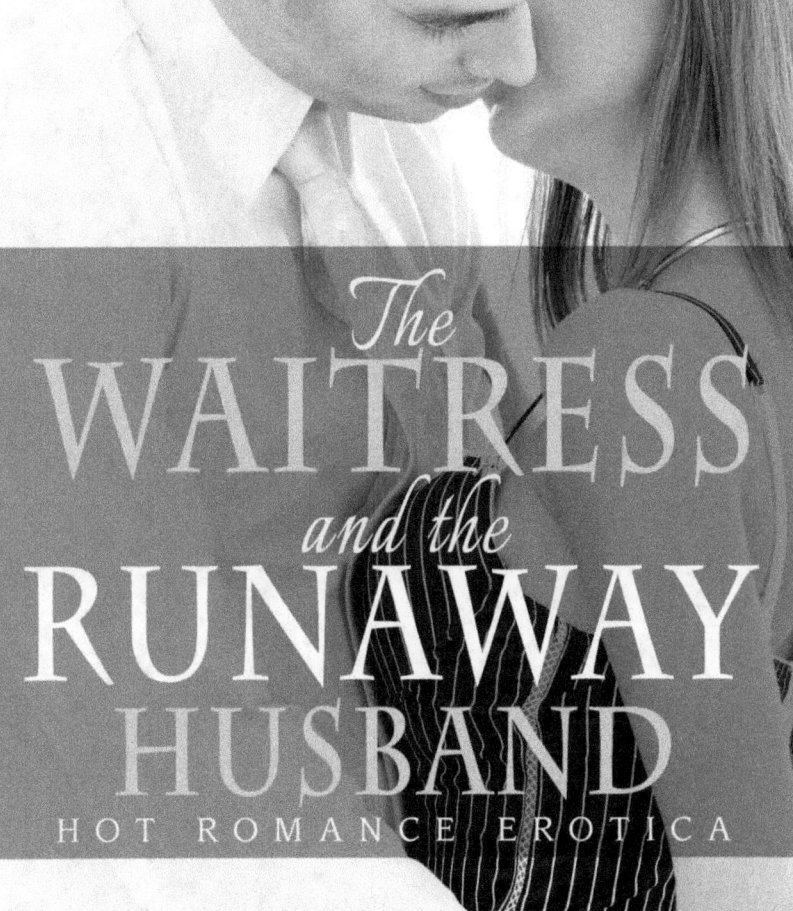

The
WAITRESS
and the
RUNAWAY
HUSBAND
HOT ROMANCE EROTICA

JUST PLAIN BOB

At check-out time I debated staying another day, but decided against it. We could always stop early in the evening and it would give me time to recharge my batteries. We had lunch at Mom's and as we ate Joyce said:

"I guess I'm still a slut. I was pretty blatant last night when I undressed wasn't I?"

"Did I look like I seemed to mind?"

"You are a guy. Guys go after pussy. I offered and so you took it."

"I guess I did didn't I? But in truth I'm not sure that I could have spent too many more nights in a room with a beautiful and sexy looking woman without trying something. And to be fair about it you yourself said you were a healthy female who had gone without for a long time. I just glad you chose me to be the one to end your long dry spell. I need to warn you though. Now that I've had a taste I'm going to want more, but if you don't you need to let me know otherwise I'm liable to take things for granted."

"Do you really think that?"

"Think what?"

"That I'm beautiful and sexy?"

"Of course I do. Why do you doubt it? Haven't you looked in the mirror lately?"

"That's different. All I see is me, but I don't see myself as others see me."

"You can take my word for it; you are both beautiful and sexy."

She smiled and said, "I think I'll stick with you. You are good for my ego."

We were on the road by twelve forty-five and we weren't ten minutes into the drive when she slid over next to me and felt for my bulge with her hand. "Have to keep you interested" she said as she found my cock and rubbed it.

"Good God woman. Can't you at least let us get a couple of hours on the road? You keep that up and I'll be pulling into the first rest area we come to."

She giggled and said, "I guess maybe I can wait that long, but if we don't come up to one soon maybe we can cut off on a side road and find a place?"

We did hit a rest area an hour later and I did pull in and park well away from anyone else. It was intense! Probably the risk factor had something to do with it. Anyone could have walked by and seen what was going on on the front seat, but I didn't care and Joyce sure didn't either. When we pulled out of the rest area Joyce slid over next to me again and I pushed her away.

"Stay on your side and at least let me drive until six or seven tonight."

"Spoil sport" she said, but she did move back to her side. After a couple of miles she took a book out of her purse and began reading it. As I drove I kept looking over at Joyce and wondered at my good fortune. What were the odds of my finding a beautiful and sexy nympho willing to pull up stakes and take of with me after knowing me less than eight hours? With luck like that I needed to stock up on lottery tickets.

We stopped at seven, checked into a motel and Joyce was peeling off her clothes before the door was fully closed. I laughed and said:

"Can't you at least wait until we have had dinner?"

"Nope. Got to work up an appetite."

We never did get to eat that night. At least not dinner.

If you enjoyed this sample then look for **The Waitress and the Runaway Husband**.

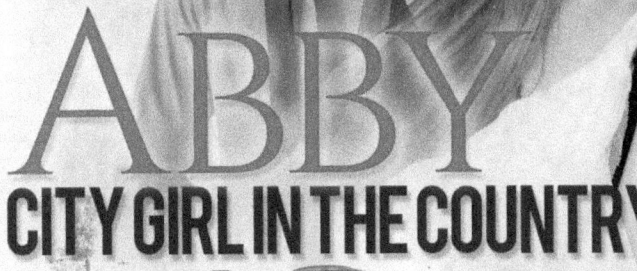

ABBY
CITY GIRL IN THE COUNTRY
EROTIC ROMANCE

KERRY JAMES

Abby had little difficulty in getting to this point, on the B3227 from Taunton heading towards South Molton, and guessed that somewhere on this road she should see a sign indicating her turn. Yet as she drove further and further into Devon she became uneasy that no such sign had revealed itself. Navigation became more of a problem as she drove deeper into the countryside, signposts, when you could find them; indicated a destination which then received no further mention at all upon succeeding signs. High banks on either side of the road meant that she had little clue as to where she was, the only point of reference was the ribbon of road unwinding ceaselessly and vanishing under the bonnet of her car and the occasional signs for some oddly named village or hamlet. As she passed through villages such as Wiveliscombe and Bampton, she wondered if she had gone wrong, and seeing the sign that said South Molton was just five miles farther on, decided that indeed she had gone wrong. Swearing mildly under her breath, Abby was giving thought to turning round and retracing her path.

Suddenly, she caught that breath; there was the sign. Leaning gently against the high banks that enclosed the road with a vigorous growth of Ivy as camouflage, she would have missed it had she not been driving slowly looking for a place to turn. It was a peculiar sensation, and her heart was beating furiously as she made the turn. A name that had previously existed only in hearsay and on a map was now a fact. Her mother had mentioned the name a few times without thinking, but would not be pressed on its significance. When her mother had died, Abby was nineteen, there was no reference at all to the name in her personal effects, which were few, there was no birth certificate, and the only official document she could find was an out of date passport, giving the birth area as South Molton. Abby's history consisted of just her mother's death certificates, and her own birth certificate. Abby now realised that she could have obtained a copy of her mother's birth certificate, but as is the way of things she had not thought logically at the time. She would repair this oversight as soon as possible. She wondered why her mum had a passport, as she had never travelled abroad.

Combe Linney, as Abby spelt it, was not even marked on her road map, and she had to resort to the Ordinance Survey to discover the location; again there was no place spelt Linney, but there was a Combe Lyney, near South Molton, and she assumed that this had to be the place. Its sum total consisted of two black oblongs, and a round dot with a cross on top, presumably indicating a church. There were no A or B roads that ventured anywhere near the place. If this wasn't the back of beyond, then it was pretty close to it.

The mystery could not be investigated immediately as Abby had after her mother's death, to consider the business of life, a job, somewhere to live. Her mother had left her little, but a stubborn trait that helped Abby survive the numerous jobs she took in the financial and insurance trade; making tea and coffee for surly men and women who viewed her simply as the office gofer.; They would have been surprised if they had known that Abby did not merely put their drinks in front of them, but closely studied what they were doing. They didn't know because Abby was invisible, unimportant, not even missed when she left to go to a better job, using all she had learned to pack her C.V. She was twenty-five when she started in the city as a proprietary equity trader, the years of watching and learning placed her in good stead. She would not say that she was a brilliant trader, there were many more that could turn sixpences into sovereigns at the drop of a hat, but she was intuitive, and with no family to call upon her time, was content to work all hours to achieve her goal. In a business where employers counted the hours almost as important as the success, she was regarded highly.

If you enjoyed this sample then look for **Abby.**

Naughty
SWINGERS

NOTHING
FORBIDDEN

STEAMY
EROTIC

George X. Bush

"Why don't we go out tonight?" Adam suggested to his wife, Keri.

"If you want to," Keri agreed. "Any special reason or place in mind?"

"Actually, yes," Adam replied. "It's a special sort of place, private."

"What's it like?" Keri asked, intrigued.

"I don't really know, except that there are special costume requirements for women," Adam told her. "I heard about it at work from some of the guys."

"What kind of special requirements?" Keri asked.

"A special mask," Adam explained.

"Where do we get it?" Keri inquired.

"Well, actually one of the guys gave me one, just in case, you know," he replied lamely.

"So, let's see it," Keri said, crooking her head sideways as she looked at her husband.

Slowly Adam reached into his briefcase and withdrew the mask.

"Oh, my," Keri said, her eyes widening in surprise as she reached for it. "This is different," she commented as she held it up and looked at it. "What is this supposed to be?" she asked, indicating a mouthpiece-like part with a ball on the other end.

"You put that part in your mouth," Adam explained.

"How do you know this?" Keri asked, a twinkle in her eye.

"They showed me how it works," Adam told her. "I didn't know either."

"So show me," Keri told him, holding it out.

"Well, it's like this," Adam said, reaching up and pulling the mask over her head. It covered her eyes and nose with the mouthpiece filling her mouth. There was a good-sized hole through the mouthpiece making it possible to breath. Adam fastened the laces in the back and tightened the mask. Now Keri couldn't see or talk and Adam noticed that her breathing rate was increasing. Keri reached up with her hands and felt around the mask, feeling the soft leather and trying to control her panic at having been stricken blind and dumb in one fell swoop. When she reached behind her head for the laces, Adam quickly untied them and helped her out of the mask.

"Wow, that's some sensation," Keri said when Adam had removed the mask. "And I'd have to wear that?"

"That's the rules," Adam told her. "If you take it off you have to leave."

"Wow! It sounds really strange," she said. "Is this something that you want to do?" Keri asked him.

"Only if you want to," Adam told her. "It sounded pretty kinky to me when they told me about it."

"They've been, obviously," Keri commented. "How did their wives like it?"

"Well, he said they'd been back since, so I guess she did," Adam replied.

"Well, if you'll take good care of me I'll go and see what it's like," Keri said, smiling at him. "What else should I wear?"

"Well, I heard there's dancing, so something comfortable for that."

"It'll be strange dancing blind," Keri commented. "But it could also be sort of neat too, I guess. Let's go change," she said, turning towards their bedroom.

It only took them about ten minutes to dress. Keri wore what she usually wore to go out dancing, a short skirt and a halter top. Her full breasts filled the halter top and her skirt came only one third of the way down her thighs. She had nice long legs and she knew she looked good. Instead of her usual high heels, though, she was wearing a pair of sensible flat shoes.

"Dancing blind, you know," she said in way of explanation.

"You look great," Adam told her, meaning it.

He thought she was the hottest looking woman on the planet and he loved it when she dressed hot to go out. As they went to the car and began driving to the party, Adam was filled with trepidation. There was more about the party that he knew that he hadn't told Keri about. He'd had this secret desire for a long time and hadn't known how to act on it until now. He just hoped that Keri would go along and not freak out.

It only took them about 20 minutes to get to where they were going, a big beautiful house in the section of the city reserved for very rich people. Keri was suitably impressed as they turned into the drive and saw about a dozen other cars already parked there. When they parked, Adam pulled out the mask and held it out to her.

"Are you sure you want to do this?" he asked once more.

"Why not?" Keri asked, taking it from him. "What's the worst that can happen?"

If you enjoyed this sample then look for **Naughty Swingers**.

THREESOMES EROTICA
DOUG AND DIANE SERIES, BOOK 1

AND MASSEUSE
Makes Three

IAN MACSWAIN

I am a professional masseuse, and have been for many years. When I say professional, I mean that I do massage strictly with no funny business, or hanky panky. My husband is a successful businessman, so I don't have to work as hard as some of my other LMT friends, but I take my work very seriously. My kids are old enough so that my not being at home when they get home from school is not an issue anymore either. This allows me the freedom to set a pretty flexible schedule.

I have a pair of clients, a husband and wife couple, that I have been massaging for quite a number of years. Doug and Diane are a very active couple with two kids in junior high school. Doug designs websites and Diane owns a floral shop. They do very nicely. Their house is up in the hills on about 10 acres of land, with a spectacular view. We have gotten very friendly over the years, like old friends. When I go to massage them, we usually sit and talk for awhile and have a glass of wine on the deck. They are such regular clients that I leave one of my massage tables at their house; they dedicated a room to it. Our relationship has always been totally professional.

Until recently.

A couple of weeks ago, I got a call from Doug, on the morning of one of our appointments, asking if he could meet me for lunch. This was a bit of an irregular request but we had become close enough client/friends that I agreed and we met at a nice restaurant near his office. We chatted for awhile, about family stuff, some business chit chat until he got around to the point and mentioned their upcoming 17th anniversary; coming up the following weekend. They had both agreed that they wanted to do something really special. Doug seemed very nervous. I asked him what was wrong.

"This is really tough to say," he stammered. "And I don't want to make you feel weird." He paused a while before continuing. "Diane and I both really enjoy your company. We think of you as a good friend, as well as our health professional." I told him that I considered them more than simply clients. "Well, we wanted to,...well, ask you if..." He trailed off again.

"I'm not following." I told him.

"We really don't want to risk our friendship with you." He said slowly. "We wanted to know if...you would consider...getting closer."

"Closer?" I asked, unsure what he meant.

"Well, at the risk of offending you, …" He was starting to hem and haw about our earlier discussion about professionalism with my work, keeping it totally professional. "We were wondering if you would consider indulging us in a more,... sensual,... kind of massage."

"More sensual?" I asked. "You mean sexual?"

"No, no." He stumbled. "Well, unless..." There was a long look between us, wherein I said nothing.

"This is not going, … you know, forget it. I'm sorry if, …" We shared a long fairly awkward silence. I think I know what he was saying, and with any other person, I would be up and out of there already. I knew these people, though. This was not something that would drive me out of my chair as I thought it might. I really liked them and Doug was really embarrassed now.

"Hey. It's okay." I told him, trying to prevent him having the heart attack he appeared to be having. I admit that I was intrigued as to what they might be considering, as a couple. It was their anniversary after all. "Just tell me what's on your mind."

"Diane was in a panic over being the one to ask, but now I wish she was here, …" I simply waited, trying not to look as flustered as I felt. I had only had to deal with these kinds of come-ons a couple of times, and had simply packed my shit and walked out; perhaps a bit stern a response but I wasn't having this discussion with strangers, men.

"Diane and I both really like you. We both think that you're awesome at what you do. And ... honestly ... we both find you very attractive, and we have both been considering ... you know ... a ... something different." Doug's hands were fluttering as if trying to not say something too outlandish. "Not that you ...", he stammered. I smiled at him.

"When I started in this line of work, I swore that I would never get involved in anything sexual with my clients." He looked a bit sad and ashamed for asking. "Don't get me wrong, I'm very flattered that you are asking. I think that you are both very attractive. Very! I suppose if I was ever to consider something like that, it would probably be with people like you two."

"But, ..." he trailed off. "I hope that you're not offended."

"No. Truly."

"I'm sorry. I really am. I hate to make you feel uncomfortable." I assured him that it was fine; that I wasn't, though secretly I was. My mind was suddenly filled with thoughts of what they might be thinking. I caught myself flashing on both their bodies. I had been their massage therapist for a while and had seen most of them already. Diane's bottom flashed into my mind, unbidden. I had to shake my head to clear it. "Will you still make our appointment tonight?"

I patted his hand. "Of course. Believe me. It's okay." He remained uncomfortable through the rest of lunch and seemed ready as hell to get out of there. The conversation was perfunctory at best; the kids' schooling, the weather; it was agony. I tried to think of something to ease his mind. I didn't want them to be embarrassed for their appointments tonight. He shook my hand rather mechanically when we stepped out onto the street, and he walked away rather briskly. I felt so bad for him. Why I didn't feel worse for myself, I don't know.

I didn't mention my lunch to my husband when I got home, as there wasn't enough time to really get into it. The kids needed feeding and then homework had to be done. I left them in front of the TV as I headed out. Later that evening when I got to their house, I felt like Diane in particular was really embarrassed. It remained that way until we were alone and I was massaging her.

I worked on her in silence until I asked, "Are you okay?"

"Yeah, I'm fine. Why?"

"You seem so quiet."

"Oh, I'm sorry. It's just that … well, I'm a little embarrassed." I asked her about what.

"Well, having Doug ask you to help us with our little … fantasy."

"Oh, please. Don't be embarrassed. Besides, we didn't really get into that much detail."

"I'm sorry for putting you on the spot like that."

"Please don't be." I told her quietly. "Besides, I'm flattered." There was a very long silence for a while, then I asked her, "I was just caught a bit… off guard." She apologized again. I just… keep my business, well… like a business." She said that she totally understood and that she hoped I wouldn't think them weird or anything. "Oh, not at all. What people do behind closed doors…" I was sounding like I was discussing it like I knew their private life. I dropped it.

There was a very long period of silence, while I continued her shoulders and back. "I just don't want you to have the wrong idea about us." She said finally.

"I don't have any idea… It's between you guys."

"It's just a stupid fantasy kind of thing." I didn't ask what. "Perhaps they are better as fantasies anyway." She said at last. I hummed that maybe so. I finished her legs and then held the sheet for her as she rolled over.

"What is your fantasy?" I suddenly blurted, not meaning to. We remained silent for awhile. She then quietly and haltingly told me how they had discussed getting a sensual massage. She was nervous about the details, so I continued to press her gently. She described a scene with soft sexy music, dim lights and lots of candles, and a sexy scene wherein a female masseuse would be topless or nude, and there would be a lot of intimate touching, between all of them. I admitted to myself that it sounded kind of cool and that my husband Josh would probably love such a thing.

She continued that Doug would help massage Diane and then vice versa. She even admitted to being curious about being with another woman. She must have talked for half an hour about what she would like to try and watch her husband try. I told her that that sounded like a magical anniversary. She admitted that maybe they should keep it as just a fantasy. I asked her if they did want to fulfill this fantasy what they would do about making it happen. She thought they might call an escort service. We left it at that.

Throughout the rest of her massage and Doug's, I kept thinking about them and the way they looked nude. Doug was silent the entire time. I was becoming intrigued with the idea of them wanting to try something new and erotic; do it together and share the experience. Even after I left their house, I couldn't get it out of my head. When I got home, the kids were asleep and Josh was reading in bed. I mentioned it to my husband, who was already half-asleep. He told me that it sounded like fun to him, and that I might enjoy it. He rolled over and turned out the light, but that comment kept me up half the night. It sounded like fun to him. And what did he mean I might enjoy it?

If you enjoyed this sample then look for **And Masseuse Makes Three**.

CHOSEN TO BE

Christy's

EXTRA LOVER

HOT SEXY EROTICA

JOAN VEGAS

As I pondered what Ben was asking me about setting up a gang bang for Christy, I knew Andy and Mark would eagerly join in. But how would I discretely recruit other guys? Ben was asking me to line up at least 6 guys, in addition to me and him. I told Ben I would try. He wanted me to set it up about 5 or 6 weeks later, when he knew he would be home. And, he told me to not mention anything to Christy about our plans. He wanted to surprise her.

A few days later, I told Mark and Andy about my mission for Christy. When I told them they would be invited, they whooped and hollered. They both said they could hardly wait. I asked if they had any suggestions on how I could line up four more guys. They both suggested other guys at our school. I wasn't so sure I wanted other guys from our school knowing about the sweet deal I had with Christy and Ben.

Then Mark suggested that we put a discrete ad in one of the local alternative newspapers that was read by younger people throughout the Chicago area. After mulling over the idea, we pooled our money to place this ad for a couple of weeks: "Pretty gal wants more than one guy...soon. Write to P. O. Box ___ for details."

To our happy surprise, one of the newspapers took our ad. A week after the paper came out, the three of us got together to open the replies we had received. Wow...9 of them. Some of them included face and/or dick pictures. I was amazed. We set aside replies from older guys and married guys. We designated four of them as good prospects.

The next week, we received eleven more replies. Most of them had understood that "The pretty gal" was looking for a gang bang. They were all eager to participate. That time, we ruled out seven of them. That left us with a total of eight prospects (not counting Mark, Andy and me). I decided to contact Ben and get his opinion before we met with any of the respondents.

Again Ben and I met for a beer...alone. I told him I had two friends who were enthusiastic about the idea of helping to fulfill Christy's wish. Then I gave him the eight envelopes we had selected. He agreed that ten guys (plus he and I) might be a bit overwhelming for Christy. He set aside three of the envelopes and said, "How about if you and your friends 'interview' these other five guys." I agreed, and we finished our beers.

That evening, Ben and I had lots of fun with Christy as we winked at each other when she was turned away, knowing what we were planning for her. We made sure she got her share of orgasms that night before we each drained our nuts inside her velvety love channel.

The next day Andy, Mark and I met. I told them about Ben's decisions. We decided on a bar where we could discretely meet with the selected guys…one at a time over the next several days. They each took two guys to call, and I took one. One of Mark's contacts proved to be a flake, so we dropped him.

Over the next week, we met individually with the four remaining guys. They all seemed clean, discrete, and personable. Most importantly, they were all very eager to share in fulfilling "Mindy's" desire to be screwed by several guys. (Yes, we changed Christy's name so no one could ever come back on her.) We got their contact phone numbers, told them the tentative time, and told them we would be calling with a hotel location where we would be meeting.

Ben arranged for a hotel suite and told Christy to be ready for an extra special evening with me and him giving her lots of passionate loving. She bought it.

Shortly after Ben and Christy arrived in the hotel room, I came in (I had my own key card). He and I necked with her while stripping off her clothes. We got her onto the middle of the large bed and Ben began to eat her. I told them I had to go get some ice for our drinks, and left Christy to enjoy Ben's oral ministrations.

I ran downstairs and met Mark and Andy. I brought them to the suite and had them quietly remove their clothes as I made noise mixing drinks for Christy and Ben. In the background, Andy and Mark were both stroking themselves to hardness. I walked into the bedroom with a drink in each hand saying, "You guys ready for some liquid refreshment?" They both sat up and reached for a drink.

Then I looked at Christy and asked, "Are you ready for some extra pleasure?" That was my cue to Mark and Andy. They walked in behind me, totally naked, with boners sticking out in front of them. I said, "Christy…this is Mark and this Andy…my friends…here to give you some extra pleasure." Christy grinned at my nude friends. Ben had already stood up. He said, "Christy baby, I hope you enjoy this special evening," and he sat in a nearby chair.

Andy dove between Christy's outstretched legs and began to lick on her pussy. Although I was still dressed, I got on the bed, cuddled Christy into my arms, and gave her a big kiss. Meanwhile, Mark laid on the bed on the other side of Christy and began caressing her body. He took one of her hands and wrapped it around his stiff dick.

Christy whispered into my ear, "What's going on?" I told her, "Tonight you are going to get your vagina eaten and screwed to your heart's content. Enjoy yourself." She grinned at me before rolling to face Mark. "You are Mark, huh?" she said, while squeezing his dick. "My," she said, "your dick is very hard. I'll bet you know how to use it." She threw her arm over his shoulder and gave him a hot kiss.

If you enjoyed this sample then look for **Chosen To Be Christy's Extra Lover.**

WANT FREE COPIES OF MY BOOKS?
Just visit my blog and download free copies of my books:
jack-ryder.awesomeauthors.org/jack-ryder